Praise for th{
Adventu{

"Young wildlife conservationist and media darling Bindi Irwin, daughter of the late 'Crocodile Hunter' Steve Irwin, is as exuberant on the pages of this peppy early reader as she is on-screen...briskly paced and delivers its message with Bindi-worthy verve."

—Publishers Weekly

"Bindi's Wildlife Adventures series creates a wonderful blend of adventure, suspense, and wildlife conservation...Children who love learning about animals and who are as devoted to saving them as Bindi and her family are will love this story and the direction of the series—a fun and educational alternative to traditional animal stories."

—New York Review of Books

"A call to action for fellow 'Wildlife Warriors,' this light and fluffy tale in the Bindi Wildlife Adventures series might appeal to those who enjoy Ben Baglio's Animal Ark and Dolphin Diaries books."

—Booklist

"In Bindi's exciting series of books, she and her friends go on adventures in a variety of places, from right at the Australia Zoo to South Africa! I recommend these books for kids ages 6 and up, especially those who love animals and want to help them."

—*Amazing Kids! Magazine*

"*Bushfire!* is a great addition to the Bindi Wildlife Adventures series...The story is interesting and slightly suspenseful, really pulling on the heartstrings and propelling us into wanting to help animals in need."

—*New York Journal of Books*

"I have one son who is an avid reader and read both [*Trouble and the Zoo* and *Rescue!*] in one sitting. He LOVED them! Another son started reading one of them and is enjoying it as well...Now our eight-year-old daughter wants to read them too... So looks like these books were a hit in our house!"

—*Laura Williams' Musings*

BOOK
8

SURFING WITH TURTLES

bindi
Wildlife Adventures

SURFING WITH TURTLES

Bindi Irwin with Jess Black

sourcebooks
jabberwocky

Published by Sourcebooks Jabberwocky, an imprint of Sourcebooks, Inc.
P.O. Box 4410, Naperville, Illinois 60567-4410
(630) 961-3900
Fax: (630) 961-2168
www.jabberwockykids.com

First published by Random House Australia in 2010.

Library of Congress Cataloging-in-Publication data is on file with the publisher.

Source of Production: Versa Press, East Peoria, Illinois, USA
Date of Production: June 2013
Run Number: 20303

Printed and bound in the United States of America.
VP 10 9 8 7 6 5 4 3 2

Dear Diary,

Surf's up, dudes! My friend Kelly and I have just had an amazing trip surfing up the west coast of Baja California in Mexico. We learned so much about the ocean, the waves, and the local marine life. We even surfed alongside green sea turtles!

The sad fact is that six out of the seven species of sea turtles are endangered. There is a huge poaching industry where people steal eggs and trade them illegally. We learned the hard way that not everyone who surfs cares about looking after marine life.

Bindi

CHAPTER ONE

With her surfboard under one arm,
Bindi stood at the water's edge, watching the waves roll in, one after another,
in glassy perfection. She felt a rush of
excitement. Here she was in Mexico,
at Los Cerritos Beach on the Baja
coast! Bindi and Kelly, her American

friend, were about to embark on a week long surf-ari, heading up the west coast, across the border, and into San Diego, California.

"Let's carve it up, dude!" Kelly was already paddling out into the surf.

"Gnarly, dude!" Bindi yelled back, giggling. The friends were having fun trying out their surf lingo!

Bindi paddled after her friend. She could just make out Kelly's spiky blonde hair as she disappeared behind a steep, feathering wave. Kelly threw herself into everything with enthusiasm, especially when it came to sports.

Once they had fought their way past the break, the friends sat on their surfboards, looking back at the shoreline. It was very relaxing bobbing up and down to the rhythm of the sea. What a view! Los Cerritos was an endless strand of soft, golden sand set against a backdrop of palm trees. The rugged desert coastline was breathtaking. It seemed a world away from the Sunshine Coast, where Bindi usually surfed.

"Did you see our itinerary?" exclaimed Kelly. "Surfing, surfing, and more surfing. This trip is going to rock!" She loved to surf and couldn't imagine anything better than a week of waves.

"Don't forget scoping out marine

life on a belly full of fish tacos!" added Bindi, who liked to get her priorities straight.

"*Muy bien*!" agreed Kelly. Bindi knew this phrase meant "very good" in Spanish. Kelly had been teaching her a few Spanish words that could come in handy for the trip.

This was more than an ordinary surf tour; it was also a marine-life adventure. Kelly shared Bindi's passion for animals and their welfare. Her family lived in Oregon and worked for Wildlife Images, a rehabilitation and education center established to care for injured wildlife. Bindi's mom, Terri, and her brother,

Robert, were spending some time in Oregon helping at the center while the lucky girls got to catch some waves.

"Out the back!" Kelly pointed to a rising swell. "This one's mine!"

Bindi watched as Kelly paddled hard until the swell lifted her board onto the wave. Then she jumped to her feet. Bindi was impressed. "Woo hoo!" she cheered on her friend.

It was Bindi's turn next, and she didn't have to wait long. A picture-perfect wave came along with her name on it. She rehearsed the steps in her head. Board lined up facing the beach. Check. Now paddle! Check.

Bindi moved her arms through the water as fast as she could to propel the board forward. It was hard work getting up the necessary speed to catch the wave before it passed her by. She felt the board lift and begin to speed up. Time to leap up! She pushed herself up to standing. She was surfing!

But then, too late, she realized her perfect little wave was too steep; the nose of her board buried itself into the wave and she was pitched forward. Wipe out!

Under the water, Bindi could feel the pitching and rolling as the wave passed over her and her leg rope gave a sharp tug to remind her she was still attached to her board. She knew enough not to fight the wave but to wait for it to pass over the top of her.

When she came up for air, Bindi swam the few strokes to her board and climbed back on. She lay still for a minute catching her breath, then began paddling toward the beach, allowing the whitewash to carry her in.

Kelly cheered her on. "Great job, Bindi!"

Bindi looked up, surprised. "But I got smashed!" she said as she stood up in the shallow water and placed her board under her arm.

"Yeah, but you did it with style!"

That was Kelly for you—always positive, always on the go.

Bindi now noticed that Kelly was standing with an older man. He had shoulder-length hair pulled back in a ponytail and a weathered face that lit up with his broad smile.

"*Buenos dias*, Bindi! I'm Matt, your teacher and guide for the next week." He was wearing a colorful surf shirt and a pair of board shorts. As they shook hands, Bindi wondered if he had seen her get dumped by the wave.

Matt gave her a smile. "Cerritos is perfect for beginners. It's got one of the nicest swells in all of Baja and is one of the more forgiving places to get dumped."

Bindi cringed. "You saw?"

Matt laughed. "It's nothing to be ashamed of. You can't learn the language of the ocean unless you let her give you a few lessons first!" He gave her a wink. "The others have arrived so we can get started. Are you ready to go out again?"

The glistening, ultramarine blue of the Pacific Ocean beckoned to her. Bindi looked over at Kelly, who was practically jumping up and down in excitement.

The two girls spoke at the same time.

"*Si!*"

"You bet!"

Matt clapped his hands together with enthusiasm. "Let's go surfing!"

CHAPTER TWO

There were three other people on Matt's surf-ari besides Bindi and Kelly. Carl and Tara were a couple in their early twenties who lived in San Diego. Adrian had a busy job at a computer company in Denver, and had always wanted to learn to surf. Having spent the morning covering basic surf theory on the sand, the five student surfers were now gathered around Matt out in the surf.

"I've been surfing all my life and I'm still learning," said Matt to the group. "In order to be a good surfer, you need to respect the ocean, her creatures, and your fellow surfers."

"Absolutely!" agreed Bindi.

"Totally!" joined in Kelly.

Tara and Adrian were nodding too. Carl looked around impatiently. "Enough with the talking. Can we do some surfing now?"

"Sure thing!" Matt leaned over

to give Carl's board a push, but Carl shrugged him off.

"I don't need your help, thanks!" Carl paddled hard, jumped to his feet, and with confidence, navigated the wave, turning this way and that as he rode it all the way to shore.

"He makes it look so easy!" Adrian complained.

"He's been surfing for years," said Tara. She watched her boyfriend admiringly. "This whole trip was a surprise. I had no idea. Carl booked the tickets and paid for the whole thing."

"Nice boyfriend," observed Kelly.

Tara smiled. "Yes, he's really special."

Bindi watched as Carl walked up the beach to join two Mexican men. They all shook hands. She thought he must be really good at making friends.

"You're up next, Bindi!" Matt motioned for her to get ready.

Bindi turned her focus to the oncoming swell and, as she scanned the horizon, she noticed a dark shadow in the water.

A very nervous Adrian noticed it too and called out to Matt. "Uh, I think we've got company."

But Bindi wasn't worried. "Hey, it's a turtle!"

They all watched as a green sea

turtle used its flippers to glide effortlessly through the water around them. Its streamlined body was the perfect shape for surfing.

"What a beauty!" exclaimed Bindi.

"You're going to have competition for the next wave, Bindi," Matt teased.

Bindi turned to see another wave approaching. She lined herself up to paddle for it. Matt gave her a push, and she caught it easily. As she surfed toward the shore, she looked down to see the turtle swimming along the same wave. A fellow surfer!

Bindi lay on her board as the wave turned to whitewash and she paddled for shore. It carried her right up to where Carl and the other two men were gathered at the water's edge. Bindi heard the end of their conversation in Spanish and thought she recognized a word.

"Did you see the turtle?" asked Bindi.

Carl looked blank.

"The one surfing my wave?" Bindi explained.

One of the men started speaking rapidly to his friend in Spanish.

Bindi was confused. "Sorry, I thought I heard you say *la tortuga.* That means turtle, right?"

Carl smiled. "You're absolutely right. I didn't know you spoke

Spanish. We did see the turtle. It was amazing!" The other men nodded enthusiastically and spoke to each other again in Spanish.

Carl turned his attention to the waves. "It's Tara's turn. This is her first ever wave. It's a big moment for her."

They all watched as Matt gave Tara a push. Tara shakily stood up on her board and began to ride the wave.

"Woo hoo!" Bindi cheered.

Carl strolled down to the water's edge to greet his girlfriend.

Bindi wanted to ask the two men if they surfed, but as she turned to speak to them, she realized they had gone.

CHAPTER THREE

Los Cerritos beach offered a stunning coral sunset over the Pacific. It was the perfect view from a hammock strung between two palm trees.

Bindi could hardly lift her arms because her shoulders were so sore from paddling. "I am so relaxed right now," Bindi sighed as she felt her body mold deeper into the hammock. Adrian was snoring in the next hammock along. Kelly was playing around with a beach ball and Tara and Carl were lying on towels on the sand.

The tranquillity was broken by Matt, who whistled to them from further down the beach, waving at them to join him. Kelly woke Adrian and the group of weary surfers made their way slowly down the beach, their muscles aching, except for Kelly, who jogged ahead to meet Matt. He led the group further along the beach and pointed out a huge leatherback turtle, an ancient-looking soul buried deep in the sand. They sat a short distance away from the turtle, admiring the colors of her shell, a scattering of gray and black blotches.

"She's a stunner!" Bindi exclaimed. She knew leatherbacks were the largest and deepest diving of the seven turtle species. They had longer front flippers than other turtles, a round body, and a short tail.

Matt was really excited. "See how she's been digging? Looks like she might be getting ready to lay some eggs."

"Don't they lay hundreds of eggs?" asked Carl.

"Yes, but unfortunately not many survive," answered Matt.

"Why not?" asked Tara.

"Because people steal them," answered Bindi.

Matt nodded. "Poachers steal the eggs. They also take hatchlings and fully grown turtles too."

"Why?" asked Adrian.

"Turtle shells are used to make jewelry and ornaments, turtle skin can be used for leather goods, and their meat and eggs can be eaten."

"I can't believe people would do that!" Tara grasped Carl's hand.

"We have to reeducate local communities so they learn to protect their endangered turtle populations."

He continued on. "Their habitat

is being destroyed by humans. Bright lights from the beach resorts confuse the hatchlings, who wander away from the water. Vehicles on the beach pack the sand down so the hatchlings can't dig their way out of their nests."

Carl shrugged. "But if you've got lots of turtles laying lots of eggs—it can't be all bad."

"I'm afraid it is, Carl," answered Matt gravely. "Six of the seven species of sea turtle are endangered. Their only predator in the ocean is the odd shark, but it's humans who have done the most damage to their population."

Bindi jumped in. "Back in

Australia, turtles confuse plastic in the ocean for jellyfish; they choke on our discarded rubbish and get tangled in fishing nets . . ." It made Bindi so mad she didn't feel able to finish her sentence.

Matt nodded gravely. "The same thing happens in Mexico and the United States. And then there are animal traffickers. People sell turtles and their eggs illegally to private owners. The border crossing between the two countries is, sadly, very popular with these types of criminals."

Tara gestured to the turtle. "How could anyone want to hurt her or her babies?"

Matt shrugged. "Money. The worst thing is that most of the animals don't even survive the journey. Each year it's estimated that 35,000 sea turtles are illegally hunted and killed throughout Baja California."

"So what can we do to help?" asked Kelly.

Matt smiled. "Well, for a start, you can join me on patrol tonight. I've volunteered to help the local turtle restoration group protect the nests from poachers."

"You can count us in," Bindi piped up, her eyes shining.

"Any other volunteers?" asked Matt.

Adrian yawned. "Would love to but I'm just too tired tonight."

Tara looked enthusiastic. She turned to Carl, who nodded slowly. "Why not?"

Matt stood up. "Excellent. I can promise you it's an amazing experience. We'd better get some dinner now and grab a few hours sleep before we get to work tonight. Okay?"

"Totally gnarly!" answered Kelly on behalf of the group. "I'm starving."

CHAPTER FOUR

Bindi awoke to the sound of a voice a few meters away.

"Bindi, Kelly, time to get up." She opened her eyes and from her hammock could see Matt packing up some gear by flashlight. It was dark and the campfire had died down to just a few embers. It took Bindi a few seconds to get her bearings, but then she remembered their expedition.

"Are you ready to join the patrol?" asked Matt.

Bindi leapt to her feet, eager to get going. "Keen as mustard, mate!"

Matt nodded to Kelly, who was fast asleep in another hammock. "She looks so peaceful. Should we let her sleep?"

Just then Kelly let out a snuffly snort in her sleep and rolled over.

"She'd never forgive me if I didn't wake her!" replied Bindi. With a cheeky grin, she walked over to

Kelly's hammock and gave it a good swing. "Wakey, wakey!"

Kelly sat up with a start, the hammock still swinging. She overbalanced and fell out of the hammock, landing on her bottom in the soft sand! Bindi and Matt couldn't help but laugh at the startled look on her face.

Bindi held out a hand to pull her up. "Sorry, couldn't resist."

Kelly grinned. "Righteous!" She jumped to her feet and dusted herself off. "But you have to know I'll get you back when you least expect it."

Bindi nodded with a glint in her eye. "Well, you can try."

Tara emerged from her tent.

"Are you and Carl ready?" asked Matt.

Tara looked half-asleep. "I thought he was with you. He couldn't sleep, so he thought he might as well be out patrolling."

Matt shook his head. "No, I haven't seen him." He handed Tara a flashlight. "We'll pair up. Tara and Kelly, you stay together, and Bindi and I will team up." Passing Kelly a walkie-talkie, he added, "It's a long beach and the last thing I want is for one of you to get lost or come face-to-face with a poacher. If you have any problems, radio me immediately."

It was a beautiful, still evening with the moon high enough to create enough light for them to make out the path. As they made their way down to the beach, Matt explained more about the night ahead.

"Once a mother lays her eggs, she'll go back to the ocean. In one season, she might do this up to seven times every nine days or so. The eggs take about two months to incubate. We're here to make sure nobody digs up any nests."

They arrived on the beach to find it was dotted with adult female leatherback turtles laying their eggs. Some were covering up nests and making their way back down the beach, their tracks visible by the moonlight.

"Wow! Amazing!" exlaimed Bindi.

Matt chuckled. "Doesn't matter how many times I see this, I'm still blown away."

Once they'd had a moment to take in the sight, Matt directed Kelly and Tara down one end of the beach. He and Bindi would patrol in the other direction.

Bindi and Matt walked in companionable silence. After about half an hour, Bindi nudged Matt to draw his attention to a figure further down the beach. The stranger was kneeling in the sand.

"What's he doing?" whispered Bindi.

Matt broke into a run. "Hey!"

Bindi followed. As they approached the man, Bindi noticed a familiar surf logo on the back of his T-shirt.

"Carl?" she called out.

The man looked around, startled. Matt and Bindi pulled up. It *was* Carl. He was kneeling down beside a turtle nest full of eggs.

"What are you doing, Carl?" asked Matt. "You know better than to touch the nests!"

Carl stood up. "I–I was just trying to help. I thought one of the eggs—" He trailed off, not sure how to continue.

Matt was really annoyed. "You should have waited for me. We don't touch the eggs. You could have done some serious damage!"

Matt kneeled down in the sand and started carefully covering over the eggs with sand. Bindi shone her flashlight on the nest so he would be able to see properly.

Carl looked around, uncertain.

After, Matt was pleased that the eggs were going to be fine, he stood up, fixing Carl with a steely gaze.

"For the rest of the night you are glued to my side. Okay?"

Carl sighed. "Understood."

CHAPTER FIVE

After a couple more hours patrolling, the group took a break at the campsite. It was almost dawn, and they were preparing to catch a few hours of sleep. Matt came back from the beach looking really excited.

"*Buenos dias*! Come and check this out!"

He led them all down to the beach where a group of local volunteers from the turtle restoration project were gathered together. They were releasing some newborn hatchlings from their hatchery.

In the dim light, Bindi and Kelly could just make out the hatchlings staggering across the sand. The tiny baby turtles crisscrossed their way down to the water and headed out to sea. The volunteers gave a cheer and the girls looked on, awestruck.

Matt addressed the group. "Don't ever forget that the volunteer work you do has a direct impact on giving these fellas a fighting chance at a life."

Bindi noticed he looked meaningfully at Carl as he spoke.

The inside of Matt's tour bus was decorated like the interior of a funky lounge room. There were surf posters on the walls, colorful curtains, and seats printed in bright Hawaiian fabric.

Bindi definitely approved. "Bonza bus!"

Matt hopped up behind the steering wheel. "Welcome to my home away from home."

Kelly asked, "Where are we going?"

"San Miguel Beach near Ensenada, just south of the border. You can practice your right turns—it's got one of the best right-hand point breaks that I know. You might even ride your first tube!"

Bindi and Kelly smiled, then both stifled a yawn.

Matt added, "It's a long bus trip, so use the time to catch up on some sleep."

The girls nodded. They were exhausted. Bindi and Kelly made

their way down the bus. They settled in at a booth complete with a table piled high with surfing and marine-life magazines.

After a good night's sleep, Adrian was flicking through some magazines. He looked up as the girls settled into their seats. "So, did you catch any nasty animal poachers last night?"

Bindi laughed. "No one apart from Carl over there."

Carl overheard the comment and grimaced. He didn't seem to appreciate the joke.

Bindi continued. "It felt good to help protect the beach though."

Adrian nodded. "I'll be sure to help out next time."

Carl and Tara took the two seats facing Bindi and Kelly. As they were settling in, the bus pulled out. Bindi was so tired, her eyelids soon grew heavy and she drifted off to sleep, her head resting on Kelly's shoulder.

Bindi had no idea how much time had passed when a cell phone rang. She stirred groggily, still half asleep. She was aware of Carl's whispered voice.

"Didn't you get my message? *La tortuga* is not going to happen."

Bindi sat up, eyes wide open. Tara was up at the front of the bus, chatting to Matt. Carl's voice grew more frustrated as the conversation continued. "Hey, I tried, man! The plan didn't work. It didn't happen!" There was silence as Carl listened to the caller. "No way! That's not what I signed up for!" At that moment, Carl looked up and realized Bindi was awake and listening to his conversation. "I guess I'll have to, won't I?" he said, lowering his voice. He hung up the phone in frustration.

"Is everything okay?" asked Tara, returning to her seat.

Carl rolled his eyes in exasperation. "AAAHH!" He ran his hands through his hair in frustration.

Kelly woke up and looked around in confusion. "What's going on?"

"Uh . . ." Carl stammered. "Ah, it's stupid. My cell phone company has got me signed up to some mega-expensive plan I never wanted. It's costing me a fortune."

"That's too bad." Tara squeezed his hand supportively.

"I'm going to have to sort it out in person. Apparently, they have an office at Ensenada." He shook his head in annoyance. "Like I so wanted to do that on my vacation."

"These things happen. Not to worry." Tara smiled at her boy-friend and ruffled his hair.

Carl relaxed a little. "Thanks, babe. It won't take long and we'll go back to enjoying our vacation, I promise."

Bindi looked out the window at the passing scenery. The view was amazing, cacti on one side and the deep blue sea on the other. But Bindi felt too unsettled to really enjoy it. Carl's behavior was making her uneasy and she didn't know why.

CHAPTER SIX

After such a long drive, everyone was glad to pile out of the bus at San Miguel Beach. Beach camping was one of the many attractions of Baja. The camping area was close to the beach and had an incredible view of the ocean. San Miguel was a legendary surf beach and Bindi was really excited about riding waves that were part of surfing history.

Bindi and Kelly were sharing a tent. The girls were experts at assembling tents—they'd shared a few family camping holidays together, and it only took a couple of minutes of teamwork to finish up. They noticed Tara struggling to put her tent up on her own.

"Need a hand?" asked Bindi.

Tara looked gratefully at Bindi. "Sure do! Carl usually helps me, but he had to go into town."

"No problem. Kelly and I can help!"

"Thanks, girls." She was looking distractedly at her pile of luggage. "I think I left something on the bus. Do you mind if I head back to look?"

Kelly and Bindi were already at work on the tent construction and waved her away good-naturedly. After setting up Tara's tent, Kelly noticed a basketball on top of Carl's luggage. She looked at Bindi with a twinkle in her eye. "How about a game?"

"Okay!" Bindi was getting used to Kelly's boundless energy, and Kelly was soon running rings around Bindi as she bounced the ball around the campsite. Bindi was trying to block her from passing when they almost collided with Carl, who was carrying a suitcase.

"Careful!" he snapped at them.

"Sorry!" said Kelly. "We're just playing a little one-on-one. Want to join us? Bindi needs all the help she can get!"

Bindi rolled her eyes.

Carl glared at them. "Is that my ball?"

"Yeah! Catch!" Kelly threw the ball to Carl who caught it with ease.

Carl didn't return the throw. He looked annoyed. "You shouldn't go through other people's stuff."

Bindi was surprised. "But we didn't. It was just–"

He shrugged, still holding on to the ball. "It's okay. Just don't let it happen again."

The girls nodded awkwardly, not sure what to do. Bindi heard a strange sound. "What was that?"

Carl looked alarmed. "What was what?"

Bindi was sure she had heard something. "That sound."

Carl started to bounce the ball. He passed it to Kelly. "I didn't hear anything."

Now Bindi was confused. "Is there air leaking out of the ball?"

Kelly looked it over. "No, the ball's fine."

Bindi was sure she heard it again. "There! Did you hear it then?"

This time Kelly was nodding. "Sure did. A bit like a hiss."

Carl laughed. "Too much sun and surf have fried your brains." He disappeared inside his tent and came back out with a rolled-up air mattress. As he squeezed the mattress, it let out a loud hissing sound.

"Here's your hiss. It's our stupid mattress. It's got a slow leak."

There was an awkward pause as Tara walked up to join them. Carl put an arm around her, all smiles.

"I grabbed your case, babe. It's in the tent."

Tara looked relieved. "Thanks, I've been looking for it. I really want to change out of these clothes."

"You don't need to do that now. Grab your board. We're going surfing."

Tara smiled. "Why not?" She headed over to grab her surfboard.

Carl turned back to Bindi and Kelly with a serious look. "Remember what I said about privacy."

After the couple had gone, Bindi turned to her friend. "There's something fishy about Carl."

"He was pretty uncool about sharing his ball," agreed Kelly.

"Mmmm," said Bindi. "I think we should keep an eye on him."

Kelly gave a mock sigh. "That means we have no choice but to go surfing." She walked over to her board and picked it up with a grin. "It's a tough life, but someone has to live it!"

CHAPTER SEVEN

After a big surfing session, Bindi fell asleep that night listening to the waves crash onto San Miguel beach. She dreamed she was surfing again with the turtle, swooping along an endless wall of water.

Bindi's dream was cut short by a

high-pitched scream. Kelly sat up at the same moment.

"What was that?" Kelly exclaimed.

"Let's find out!" Bindi was already unzipping their tent flap. They stumbled out of the tent toward the sound.

Adrian and Matt were also outside, running across the campsite toward Carl and Tara's tent. Bindi and Kelly followed.

"Tara, what's going on?" Matt called out. As they reached the tent, the screaming died down to a muffled whimper. Bindi and Kelly exchanged a look. What was Carl doing?

The sound of whispering was

followed by Carl stepping outside. "Sorry, guys. Tara's fine. She had a nightmare. She sometimes gets night terrors."

"She certainly sounded terrified." Matt looked less than convinced of Carl's story.

"Yeah, well, they're really scary," replied Carl.

"Is there anything we can do?" Bindi asked.

"Just go back to bed. It's fine."

Matt folded his arms and didn't move. "I'm not leaving this spot until I see that Tara is okay."

Carl held out his hands to placate Matt. "Chill out, man!" He leaned back into the tent entrance. "Babe, you've got a posse of concerned fans out here who aren't going to get any sleep until they see that you are okay."

There was silence followed by some rustling before Tara stepped out of the tent. She was deathly pale and her hands were shaking.

"You look like you need a hug!" said Bindi, and she threw her arms around Tara. "Are you sure you're okay? Your heart is beating really fast!"

Tara avoided looking at the others but whispered to Bindi, "Thanks for checking on me."

Carl drew Tara to him and kept his arm around her waist. "You're fine now. Aren't you, babe?"

She nodded.

"If you need anything, I'm right here in the next tent," Matt said to Tara.

"Show's over, folks." Carl looked defiantly at Matt. *"Buenos noches."* He led Tara back into the tent and zipped the tent shut with finality.

"I guess that's good night then." Matt walked back to his tent and the others did the same.

Bindi and Kelly lay in the dark, but neither of them felt ready to go back to sleep.

Kelly giggled. "Turtles one night, screaming girls the next. We're not getting much sleep on this tour, are we?"

Bindi snorted. "It's not the endless summer; it's the endless sleepover!"

Both girls hugged their pillows and lay in silence.

Bindi couldn't escape her uneasy feeling. "Tara looked really scared," she whispered.

Kelly nodded in agreement and rolled over to look at her friend. "What should we do?"

"There's not much we can do now with Carl around, but let's keep our ears open in case Tara needs us."

The two friends sat back to back, keeping each other awake. It was going to be a long night.

CHAPTER EIGHT

It was hard to believe they were on the final leg of their trip. Once they crossed the border, there were only two more days of surfing. Matt would be taking them to some of his favorite breaks around San Diego.

Bindi was really looking forward to seeing her mum and Robert again.

Kelly's mom, Sarah, Terri, and Robert would be in San Diego to meet them. Both girls were missing their families. The mood between the group had been uncomfortable all morning. Tara had hardly spoken and there was tension between Matt and Carl.

They were loading up the bus when Tara approached Bindi and Kelly. "I just came to say good-bye."

Bindi was surprised. "But we're on our way to San Diego. Isn't that your home?" She noticed Carl was hovering nearby, listening to their conversation.

"I'm not sure anymore." Tara gave a tight smile. "That's up to Carl."

Carl looked nervously at the girls

and then back at Tara. He lowered his voice. "I've got no choice."

"You always have a choice," replied Tara.

Tara gave Bindi and Kelly a quick hug. "I might head back down to the turtle sanctuary and do some volunteer work."

She gave Matt a wave. "Maybe see you there."

He nodded. "Take care of yourself, Tara."

Bindi noticed Tara's suitcase over by the other bags. "What about your stuff?"

Tara shook her head. "I can do without that kind of baggage

in my life." She turned and made her way down the beach without a backward glance.

It wasn't far to the border, just over an hour by bus. During the journey, Bindi couldn't stop thinking about Carl's strange behavior: digging up the eggs; his suspicious phone call on the bus; his overreaction to them playing with his basketball; not to mention Tara leaving him. What did it all add up to? What did Carl have to hide?

The compression of the air brakes squeaked and hissed as the bus slowed down to join the queue of traffic at the border crossing between Mexico and the United States.

The noise of the brakes reminded her of...All of a sudden Bindi knew what Carl was up to! She turned to Kelly and whispered, "Carl's about to do something very silly and we have to stop him!"

Both girls twisted around in their seats to face Carl. He was staring at the suitcase on the seat next to him.

"Don't do it, Carl," said Bindi.

Kelly wasn't sure what was going on but she trusted Bindi.

Carl didn't even look at them; it was as if he hadn't heard Bindi speak.

"It's not worth going to jail for or losing the people you love," she continued.

Carl looked desperate. "What would you know? You're just a kid." He twisted the strap of the suitcase nervously in his hand.

Bindi glanced at the suitcase with concern. "People could get hurt."

Carl's hands fidgeted more as she spoke. "You can still change your mind."

Carl now looked really scared. "It's too late!" As he spoke, his hands repeatedly twisted the buckles of the suitcase. Bindi could see what was going to happen.

"Be careful of the strap, Carl!"

Too late. The suitcase burst open and just as Bindi had suspected, inside was a very annoyed, hissing snake.

CHAPTER NINE

Adrian screamed as the red, black, and cream-striped snake reared its head out of the suitcase and hissed angrily.

"What's going on?" Matt called out from the driver's seat.

"You better get back here," Kelly called to him.

Bindi took charge of the situation.

"Kelly, I need you to get Adrian off the bus. No fast movements."

"Sure thing."

Kelly led the shaking Adrian slowly down the aisle toward the front door of the bus.

Carl sat frozen, staring at the snake. "If this coral snake bites me, I'll die!"

Bindi moved very slowly out of her seat toward the snake. "They're not naturally aggressive, but it looks pretty angry right now. Can't say I blame it."

Carl looked like he might faint. The snake was still lunging forward, hissing at him.

Bindi slowly held out her hands. "It's okay, beautiful fella. I'm not going to hurt you. You've had a rough time, haven't you? It's okay now. I'll look after you. Ssshh." Bindi inched closer and closer. The snake didn't react as strongly to her but gave her a warning hiss.

"I think you should back away, Bindi. I can handle this," said a nervous Matt, adding, "Their venom is deadly."

Bindi inched closer. Her right hand could almost touch the snake, and she was definitely within striking distance. "Don't come any closer, Matt. You'll spook him."

Matt was unsure how to handle the situation, but he didn't want Bindi getting hurt. He took a step closer to the snake. The snake lashed out and almost struck Carl in the arm.

"I'm so outta here." Carl took the chance to make a dash for it and was out of his seat before Matt could stop him. Anyway, his main worry was getting Bindi to safety. She seemed completely unfazed and kept murmuring soothing words as she made eye contact with the reptile.

Time stood still. Dimly in the distance, Bindi could hear car horns beeping and the sound of voices outside. She was aware that Matt stood very close to her. But for Bindi, there was nothing but her and the snake. Her focus was complete.

"Come on, little fella. I'm not going to hurt you. I want to take you home." She was transfixed by his beautiful markings, the red, black, and cream stripes that crossed his body. What was that rhyme again? she thought as she and the snake locked eyes. *Red next to black, posion I lack; red next to yellow, run away, fellow.* This wasn't a coral snake but a Mexican milk snake. Their colorful markings were really similar, and people often confused the two. He was angry, that was certain, but he wasn't venomous.

Bindi stretched her arm out just a little further. Here was her moment. She reached out and grabbed the snake by the tail. She maintained a grasp despite his writhing and hissing. And with both hands firmly holding the snake, Bindi gently placed him back into the suitcase.

"Matt, could you please close the lid?" she asked calmly.

Matt moved behind her well out of the snake's reach, and lowered the lid of the case.

Bindi apologized to her new reptilian friend. "I'm sorry, gorgeous.

I promise I will get you home." She firmly rebuckled the straps on the case.

Bindi glanced out the window. Kelly was jumping up and down, trying to see what was going on inside the bus. Bindi smiled to her and gave her the thumbs up. Kelly broke into a mini cheerleading routine in celebration.

Matt let out a deep sigh. "Respect!" He looked at Bindi with admiration. "You are one radical girl, Bindi!"

Bindi smiled. "The poor milk snake was more scared of us than we were of him."

Matt laughed and sank down into a seat. "Speak for yourself, little lady!"

It turned out that Carl didn't get as far away as he would have liked. Two Mexican border officials in starched uniforms were waiting for him as he exited the bus.

Carl looked a sorry sight, waiting in handcuffs. He looked up when Bindi and Matt stepped off the bus. "I've really messed up."

Matt was angry. "You sure have.

The sad fact is that I've seen your kind far too often before. I tipped these guards off. Even if the snake hadn't escaped, you would never have made it across the border."

Carl let out a defeated groan. "I got this offer to make really good money if I delivered turtle eggs to this guy across the border in the States. When I couldn't deliver on that, they forced me to pick up this snake to deliver to some private collector. I'd already been partly paid, so I had to do what they said. They threatened me."

"Not such nice people to do business with, then?" Matt commented.

"Was Tara involved too?" Bindi was concerned for her friend.

Carl sighed. "Tara didn't know anything. She discovered the snake in her suitcase the night she screamed the campsite down. And she didn't want to stay with me after that."

The guards were starting to look impatient. Matt gave them the nod. "Time to go, Carl."

Carl seemed resigned to his fate. "For what it's worth, Matt, I'm sorry."

Matt shrugged. "We're not the ones you should be apologizing to."

Carl met Bindi's eyes and then hung his head. The guards led him away.

CHAPTER TEN

It was their last day of surfing together and the conditions were just perfect at La Jolla Shores, outside San Diego. It was a beautiful spot with loads of marine life—seals, guitar fish, leopard sharks, lobsters, and more turtles! Wave after gentle wave rolled into the shore. At La Jolla Shores, even the palm trees seemed relaxed.

Adrian, Kelly, Matt, and Bindi were sitting on their boards out-the back, waiting for the next wave. They took in the view of the rugged cliffs, natural coves, and rock formations. It sure was a stunning place.

Bindi could see her mum, Sarah, and Robert on the beach watching. It had been so good to see them again. She thought about Carl. He'd traded in the person he loved for a business deal. He'd allowed an animal to suffer for his greed. And now, as a result, he was in serious trouble.

"The next wave's mine!" Bindi announced. "And for the record, I'm going to totally carve it up!"

The others laughed as Bindi lined herself up and paddled as furiously as she could.

"Go, girl!" she could hear Kelly calling to her as she plowed her arms through the water. Just when she thought she might have missed it, the gentle rise of the swell propelled her forward. Bindi could feel the shape of the wave—her timing was just right.

"Bingo!" Bindi did her best snap to standing and soon she was dropping down the face of the wave.

Everything came together—the board and her body channeling the power of the wave. She sped along the wall of water, enjoying the sea spray in her hair, the sun on her face.

As Bindi looked down at the water, she saw a green sea turtle surfing alongside her, enjoying the wave as much as she was.

"Woooo hooooo!" she yelled. It was the perfect wave to share with a friend.

THE GREEN SEA TURTLE

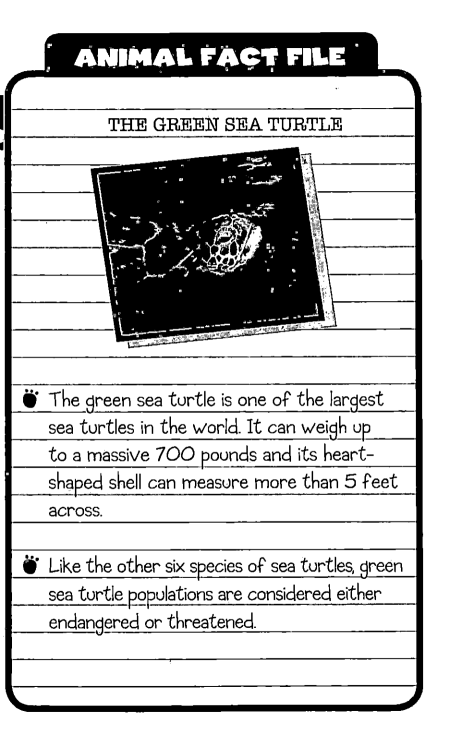

🐾 The green sea turtle is one of the largest sea turtles in the world. It can weigh up to a massive 700 pounds and its heart-shaped shell can measure more than 5 feet across.

🐾 Like the other six species of sea turtles, green sea turtle populations are considered either endangered or threatened.

- All species of turtles have evolved a bony outer shell that protects them from predators, as turtles are not known for their speed.

- When active, sea turtles swim to the surface every few minutes in order to breathe. When sleeping or resting, which usually occurs at night, adult sea turtles can remain underwater for more than two hours without breathing.

- Green sea turtles get their name from the color of their body fat, which is green because of the algae they eat.

- Adult green sea turtles are herbivores, while juvenile green sea turtles are carnivorous. Their diet consists of jellyfish and other invertebrates.

● Although green sea turtles live most of
their lives in the ocean, adult females must
return to land in order to lay their eggs.
This is done at night. Once the clutch of
up to 100 eggs has been laid, the mother
returns to the ocean and the young have
to fend for themselves.

● Green sea turtles are fast and powerful
swimmers, reaching speeds of
nearly 40 miles per hour.

ANIMAL FACT FILE

THE MEXICAN MILK SNAKE

- The Mexican milk snake is a type of king snake. There are about 25 different species of milk snakes in the world.

- The Mexican milk snake is native primarily to northeastern Mexico in Coahuila, Tamaulipas, and Nuevo León, but it can be found as far north as the United States, in southwestern Texas.

- The milk snake will grow between 20 to 60 inches long.

- They have very smooth and shiny scales, with a pattern that alternates bands of red, yellow, and black, which can be mistaken for the venomous coral snake.

- Mexican milk snakes are generally nocturnal and prefer to rest during the hotter parts of the day.

- The milk snake is an opportunistic feeder and will eat a wide and varied assortment of prey items, including slugs, insects, earthworms, lizards, birds, and small mammals.

- Milk snakes lay an average of about 10 eggs per clutch.

Become a Wildlife Warrior!

Find out how at www.wildlifewarriors.org.au

Bindi says: "It is important to promote the non-consumptive use of wildlife. We need to stop killing, and start protecting our wildlife."

TROUBLE
AT THE ZOO

BOOK 1

Bindi's birthday party at the zoo is going to be HUGE. Karaoke, animal rides, dancing contests—it's all going on! But when a spoiled ten-year-old boy decides he wants to take home one of the zoo's precious water dragons, Bindi, her brother Robert, and a green-winged macaw come to the rescue. Can Bindi save the water dragon and her party?

RESCUE!

Bindi and her friend, Hannah, are on a horse-riding trek in South Africa to see the amazing wildlife. While on their trip, the girls discover that a nature preserve for the giant sable antelope is being used for illegal hunting at night. When Bindi and Hannah try to help, they get caught spying. Will Bindi and Hannah get a chance to tell anyone what's going on and save the antelope?

BOOK 2

BUSHFIRE

While on an early morning walk, Bindi and her best friend, Rosie, see smoke on the horizon. It's a terrible bushfire! As fire spreads across the national park, the girls know they must do something. They rush to the Australian Wildlife Hospital to help care for animals that were trapped in the fire. So many animals were hurt! Can they save a mama koala and her baby joey?

BOOK 3

CAMOUFLAGE

Bindi and her family are visiting Singapore for the opening of a new reptile park. It's going to be so much fun! But when a rare Komodo dragon is missing, Bindi and her brother Robert have to blend into their surroundings to find her. Will they solve the mystery and save the beautiful lizard before the grand opening of the park?

BOOK
4

A WHALE OF A TIME

BOOK 5

Bindi takes a pair
of troublesome twins on a
thrilling whale-watching trip. It's
going great until one of the twins spots
a bright flare in the sky. They race
to the scene and find an oil spill! Can Bindi
help stop the oil leak and save the nearby
whales from danger?

ROAR!

Bindi and her family are on their way to the jungle to collect three cute tiger cubs to take back to Australia Zoo. Soon after meeting the playful cubs, Bindi and her new friend, Madi, learn that the tigers in a nearby park are in danger from thieves! Can the two friends track down the gang before they nab the tigers?

CROC
CAPERS

Bindi and her
family are on their annual
trip to study crocodiles. The
nature reserve is a beautiful place, but
with all the crocodiles around, it can be
dangerous too. So when Bindi and Robert
stumble upon a mysterious campsite, they
decide to check it out. Are the campers in
trouble—or up to no good?